By Jane Thayer • Illustrated by Lisa McCue

HarperCollins*Publishers*

The Puppy Who Wanted a Boy

www.harperchildrens.com
The Puppy Who Wanted a Boy was previously published
in 1988 by Mulberry Books.

Library of Congress Cataloging-in-Publication Data
Thayer, Jane.
The puppy who wanted a boy.
Summary: When Petey the puppy decides that he wants
a boy for Christmas, he discovers
that he must go out and find one on his own.
ISBN 0-06-052696-3 — 0-06-052697-1 (lib. bdg.)
[1. Dogs—Fiction. 2. Christmas—Fiction.]
McCue, Lisa, ill. II Title.
PZ7.T3297Pu 1986 [E] 85015465

Typography by Adriana Cordero
1 2 3 4 5 6 7 8 9 10
❖

First Mulberry Edition, 1988
First HarperCollins Edition, 2003

One day Petey, who was a puppy, said to his mother, who was a dog, "I'd like a boy for Christmas."

His mother, who was a dog, said she thought he could have a boy if he was a very good puppy.

So the day before Christmas Petey's mother asked, "Have you been a very good puppy?"

"Oh, yes!" said Petey. "I didn't frighten the cat."

"You didn't?" asked Petey's mother.

"Well-l, I just frightened her a *little*," said Petey. "And I didn't chew any shoes."

"Not *any*?" said his mother.

"Just a teeny-weeny chew," said Petey. "And I remembered—well, almost always remembered—to bark when I wanted to go out."

"All right," said his mother. "I think you've been good for such a little dog. I will go out and get you a boy for Christmas."

But when Petey's mother came back she looked very worried. "How would you like a soft white rabbit with pink ears for Christmas?" she said to Petey.

"No thanks," said Petey.

"Don't you want a lovely canary?"

"I'd like a boy," said Petey.

"How about some guppies?" said Petey's mother.

"I just want a boy," said Petey.

"Petey," said his mother at last, "there are no boys to be found."

"No boys?" cried Petey.

"Not one could I find. They're terribly short of boys this year."

Petey thought he couldn't stand it if he couldn't have a boy.

Finally his mother said, "There now, there must be a boy somewhere. Perhaps you can find some dog who would give his boy away."

“Do you think I could?” asked Petey.

“It wouldn’t hurt to try,” said his mother.

So Petey started off. It wasn’t long before he saw a collie racing with a boy on a bicycle. Petey trembled with joy.

“If I had a boy on a bicycle,” said Petey to himself, “I could run like anything! I’ll take a little run right now, and I’ll ask the collie politely if he’ll give his boy away.”

So Petey leaped after the bicycle. He called out to the collie, "Excuse me. Do you want to give your boy away?"

But the collie said no, he definitely didn't, in a dreadful tone of voice.

Petey sat down. He watched the collie and his boy on a bicycle, until they were out of sight.

"I didn't really want a boy on a bicycle anyway," said Petey.

After a while he saw a setter playing ball with a boy. Petey was delighted. “If I had a boy to play ball with,” said Petey, “I’d catch the ball smack in my mouth. I’d like to catch the ball now.”

But he remembered how cross the collie had been. So he sat down on the sidewalk and called out politely, “Excuse me. Do you want to give your boy away?”

But the setter said no, he definitely didn’t, in a terrifying tone of voice!

“Oh well, said Petey, trotting off, “I don’t think playing ball is so much fun.”

Soon Petey came to a bulldog, sitting in a car with a boy. Petey was pleased, for he was getting a little tired from so much walking.

"If I had a boy in a car," said Petey, "I'd laugh at walking dogs. I'd like a ride right now."

So he called out loudly, but very politely, "Excuse me. Do you want to give your boy away?"

But the bulldog said no, he definitely didn't, and he growled in Petey's face.

“Uh-oh!” said Petey. He hurried behind a house and stayed there until he saw the bulldog and his boy drive away.

“Well, who wants to go riding in a car? Not me!” said Petey, coming out from behind the house.

He thought he would just rest a while, though. He had come a long way for such a little dog. He was limping a bit when he started off again. After a while he met a Scottie, walking with his boy and carrying a package in his mouth.

"Now that is a good kind of boy!" said Petey. "If I had a boy to take walks with and carry packages for, there might be some dog biscuits or cookies in the package. I would like a cookie right now!" He hadn't had any lunch.

But he remembered how cross the collie and the setter and the bulldog had been. So he stayed across the street and shouted at the top of his lungs, but polite as could be, "Excuse me. Do you want to give your boy away?"

The Scottie had his mouth full with the package. But he managed to say no, he definitely didn't, and he showed his sharp teeth to Petey.

HOME
FOR BOYS

"I guess that wasn't the kind of boy I wanted either," said poor Petey. "But my goodness, where *can* I find a boy?"

Well, Petey trotted on and on. But he couldn't find a single dog who would give his boy away. Petey's ears began to droop. His tail grew limp. His little legs were *very* tired. My mother was right, he thought. There isn't a boy to be found.

Just as it was getting dark, he came to a large building on the very edge of town. Petey was walking by slowly when he saw a sign: HOME FOR BOYS.

"Maybe I can find a boy here!" said Petey to himself. "These boys have no parents, and no dog to take care of them either." He padded slowly up the walk of the Home. He was so tired he could hardly lift his little paws.

Then Petey stopped. He listened. He could hear music. He looked through the window. He saw a lighted Christmas tree, and children singing carols.

Then Petey saw something else. On the front steps of the building, all by himself, sat a boy! He was not a very big boy, and he looked lonely.

Petey gave a glad little cry. He forgot about being tired. He leaped up and landed in the boy's lap. Sniff, sniff, went Petey's little nose. Wag, wag, went Petey's tail. He kissed the little boy with his warm, wet tongue. How glad the boy was to see Petey! He put both his arms around the little dog and held him tight.

Then the front door opened and a lady looked out. "Why, here you are, Ricky!" she said. "What is our newest boy doing out here all alone? Come on in and sit near the Christmas tree."

Petey sat very still. The boy sat still. The boy looked up at the lady and down at Petey. Petey began to tremble. Would the boy go in and leave him?

"I'm not alone," said the boy, "I've got a puppy."

"A puppy!" The lady came out and looked at Petey in surprise.

"Can he come, too?" said the boy.

"Why," said the lady, "you're a nice little dog. Wherever did you come from? Yes, bring him in."

"Come on, puppy," cried the boy. In they scampered!

A crowd of boys was playing around the Christmas tree. They rushed at Petey. They picked him up and petted him.

Petey wagged his tail. He wagged his fat little body. He frisked about and licked every one of the boys.

33

“Can we keep him?” said one.

“Can we give him some supper?” said another.

“Can we fix him a nice warm bed?” said a third.

“We will give him some supper and a nice warm bed,” said the lady. “And tomorrow we will find his mother and see if she’ll let him stay.”

Petey knew his mother would let him stay. She knew how much he wanted a boy. "But won't she be surprised," said Petey to himself, with a happy little grin, "when I tell her I got *fifty* boys for Christmas!"